For Navid and Justin
Marije Tolman

Text copyright © 2006 by Lida Dijkstra
Illustrations copyright © 2006 by Marije Tolman
Originally published under the title *Schattig*
by Lemniscaat b.v. Rotterdam, 2006
All rights reserved
Printed in Belgium
First U.S. edition, 2007

Library of Congress Cataloging-in-Publication Data is available.

LEMNISCAAT
An Imprint of Boyds Mills Press, Inc.
A Highlights Company
815 Church Street
Honesdale, Pennsylvania 18431

Cute

Lida Dijkstra

ILLUSTRATIONS BY
Marije Tolman

Lemniscaat
Asheville, North Carolina

Toby was a soft, fuzzy, and very cute rabbit.
Everybody said so.

He hated that! So he decided to change his image.

Toby put on shiny sunglasses. He puffed out
his chest and practiced a new walk. He felt very cool.
The other animals laughed. "Look at Toby,"
they said. "He is so cute!"

Toby had to do something quick. He pierced his ear and tattooed his arm.

Back on the street, Toby growled softly as he strutted around.

His friends shook their heads. Owl said, "Toby is making a fool of himself."

The others didn't say a thing.

I am on the right track! Toby thought.

He had a brilliant idea for sealing his new image.

He popped a wheelie on his new noisy motorbike.
His friends plugged their ears as he tore dangerously
down the street. His cape flapped behind him.
Finally, he thought, *I am not cute anymore.*

Toby barely stopped in time at the Zebra crossing.
Tara was frightened when she saw him.
Toby looked at Tara. *She is soft, fuzzy, and very cute,* Toby thought. "Hey, baby," he said.
Tara sniffed at him. "Get lost, creep," she said.

She danced away.

Creep?

In a flash Toby got rid of all his cool stuff ...

and hopped after Tara. He was too shy to talk to her, but he felt very happy.

The next day Toby brought beautiful flowers to Tara.
At first, Tara did not recognize Toby. She stared at him.
He is soft, fuzzy, and very cute, she thought.

Toby and Tara decided to share everything. They fit perfectly together in one chair. They had one house, one stove, and one pot of carrots. There was one of everything until spring when twelve baby rabbits were born. The baby rabbits were small and fuzzy. And, of course, they were very …

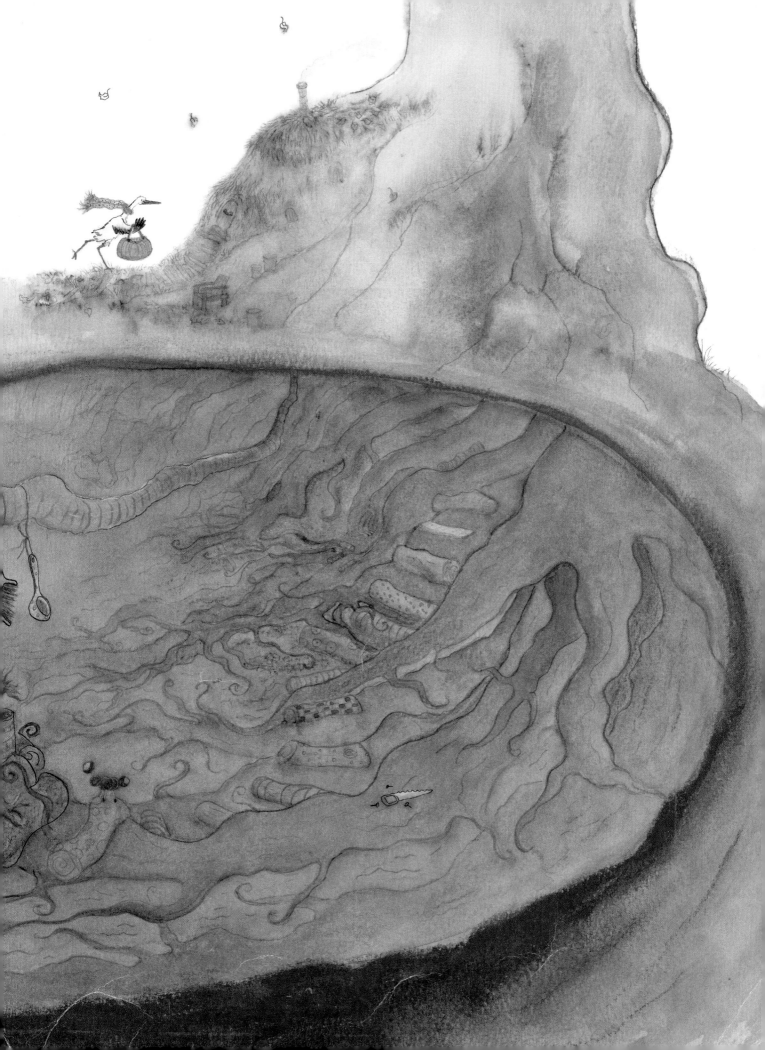

NAUGHTY!